The Adventures of Badger's Set

The animals in the wood were bored and bad-tempered. 'Something,' said Badger, 'has got to be done.' As he was good at organizing things, Badger called a meeting. 'Ladies and Gentlemen,' he said, 'suggestions please. The floor is yours.'

There was much giggling and shuffling, and the only real suggestion came from Tortoise. 'When I was a pet, and lived in a house, I remember there was a great deal of interest in all sorts of sporty things, like games, and competitions, and I . . .'

The animals cheered with delight. 'We can have running, and jumping, and sliding down the muddy hill . . .'

'Brilliant, Tortoise!' roared Badger. 'What an absolutely splendestible idea! We can call it . . . how about . . . Badger's Olympical Games!'

From then on life was anything but boring. Tortoise was desperate to win a gold medal, but could he beat hare at running and frog at jumping . . . ?

And then there was the time when Hedgehog found the fairy ring and wished a wish that came true . . . And the terrible fire that swept through the wood, from which Tortoise emerged a hero!

The adventures of Badger, Tortoise, Hedgehog and company are funny and endearing, and the lively black and white illustrations by Lesley Smith add their own particular magic to the story.

The Adventures of Badger's Set

Emil Pacholek

Illustrated by Lesley Smith

A Hippo Book
Scholastic Publications Ltd
London

Scholastic Publications Ltd, 161 Fulham Road,
London SW3 6SW England
Scholastic Book Services, 50 West 44th Street,
New York 10036 NY, USA
Scholastic Tab Publications Ltd, 123 Newkirk Road,
Richmond Hill, Ontario L4C 3G5, Canada
H J Ashton Co Pty Ltd, Box 579, Gosford, New South
Wales, Australia
H J Ashton Co Pty Ltd, 9-11 Fairfax Avenue, Penrose,
Auckland, New Zealand

First published by
Scholastic Publications Ltd 1980
Copyright © Emil Pacholek 1980
Illustrations copyright © Lesley Smith 1980
All rights reserved

Made and printed in Great Britain by
Hazell Watson & Viney Ltd,
Aylesbury, Bucks
Set in Baskerville

Badger's Olympical Games!

ONCE, WHEN ALL THE creatures of the forests and the woodlands were feeling rather bored, they met in a clearing to decide what to do to make life more interesting.

Badger, who in his opinion was the most important creature in the entire world, chaired the meeting.

He tapped on a tree trunk for silence, then drew in a huge breath that tightened every button on his waistcoat.

'Gentlemen,' he announced, in his most dignified voice.

Mrs. Squirrel in the second row, coughed.

'Er . . . *Ladies* and Gentlemen,' Badger corrected himself, 'I think I can safely say, without fear of further interruption, that we are well and truly bored . . .'

'Then you must be Chairman of the Bored!'

chuckled Hedgehog. 'Get it? You're the chairman, and we're all bored, get it, eh?'

Badger, who didn't particularly like jokes, especially the kind Hedgehog liked to make, was not amused. He looked over the top of his spectacles and sighed.

'Oh, really—must we?' he said in a tired sort of way.

Hedgehog curled up into a ball and remained like that for quite some time.

Badger began yet again.

'What we need is an interest, something to occupy ourselves, something to prevent the periglimations of the mind!'

This was typical Badger, using a word like 'periglimations'. No one had ever heard such a grand-sounding word before. And little wonder, for it was one of Badger's invented words—the sort he often made up, just to impress.

And, what's more, impress it jolly well did, for several murmurs of 'hear, hear' and 'well said' were heard to come from the assembled animals.

Chairman Badger paused, looked around, and when he was quite sure that he'd impressed everyone, he continued.

'And now, Ladies and Gentlemen, one at a time, please, may I have your suggestions?'

A branch in a tall oak tree creaked. A nearby stream made a noise like little silver bells tinkling on a soft summer's breeze. But no one spoke.

No one.

Then Tortoise, who'd been a pet before he'd wandered off into the woodlands, stood up.

Slowly.

Very slowly.

'Em . . . Mr. Chairman?' he ventured, ever so politely. 'May I . . . may I say a word . . . em . . . if you don't mind?'

'Tortoise, the floor is yours,' declared Badger grandly, pushing his spectacles back up his snout as he sat down.

'Em . . . well . . .' said Tortoise. 'When I was a pet . . . that is to say, when I lived in a house . . .'

'Oh no, we're not getting all that rubbish again!' groaned Hedgehog, who'd heard Tortoise start so many tales this way.

'Quiet, please!' grunted Badger, and Hedgehog curled up again.

'Well . . . anyway . . . when I lived in a house,' went on Tortoise, 'I remember there was a great deal of interest in . . . em . . . all sorts of sporty things, like games and . . . competitions, and I was wonder—'

'Brilliant, Tortoise!' came the sudden roar from

Badger. 'A competition! What an absolutely splen-destible idea!'

There were more murmurs of 'hear, hear' and then someone clapped.

'We can have running!' shouted someone.

'And jumping!' cried another.

'And ski-ing down the muddy hill!'

'And throwing the stone!'

Badger broke in. 'Yes . . . yes . . .' he exclaimed, 'We can call it ... how about ... Badger's Olympical Games!'

And suddenly the entire meeting burst into cheering. It was a good idea!

Hares and rabbits and mice and frogs a squirrels and hedgehogs and moles and voles a all the animals were on their feet and clapp and jumping and dancing and hugging other.

Yes, it was a great idea!

And from that moment on, all the creat the forests and the woodlands had an in life.

Badger's Olympical Games!

And although the whole idea had be by Tortoise, Badger took it over as if i his very own! But Tortoise didn't Badger was so good at organizing t better than he was, really.

And besides, Tortoise had other things on his mind. Much more important things.

Like how on earth could he win a medal? For that was what he wanted more than anything else in the whole wide world—to win a medal in Badger's Olympical Games.

Before he tucked his head into his shell to go to sleep that night, Tortoise looked up at the moon and the stars for a long, long time.

And wished.

THE MOLES WERE GIVEN the task of making the stadium. First of all, they removed all the stones and the fallen branches and the twigs and the leaves and the 'things' from the middle of the clearing.

And when the oval-shaped arena had been marked off with little flags and pegs and string, they banked up heaps and heaps of earth until it was piled high enough to hold the crowds of spectators at the Games.

Some moles were diggers and some were scrapers. And some were pilers and some were rakers. And some were shovellers and others wheeled squeaky-wheeled wheelbarrows.

And when the hours of daylight were not long enough, the moles worked late into the night as well—by the flickering light of a thousand glow-worms clustered in the trees around them.

Once the centre of the stadium had been rolled perfectly flat and even, they made a running-track, a jumping-pit, and a specially fenced-off area for the Throwing the Stone event.

And down the slope beyond the far end of the arena, they created the ski run. It started at the top of a muddy bank and finished, after twisting and winding its way down the hill, right slap-bang in the centre of the stadium.

13

'A brilliant piece of diggifications!' as Badger called it.

And all this was done in only five days and five nights.

The moles were not the only ones who were working hard.

So was Tortoise.

In another part of the forest, far away from everyone, he was busy training—getting himself in trim for the Games.

He really looked like a sportsman, with his shorts, vest, and shoes. He even had a stop watch to check his running times!

'Right,' he said to himself. 'Now for a quick sprint to that . . . em . . . tree and back. Shouldn't take a minute.'

Tortoise crouched down, the way real runners do.

'Ready,' he whispered.

'Steady,' he whispered.

'Go!'

But his poor old legs just wouldn't move fast enough. By the time he staggered back to his stop watch, it had taken him not one minute—but ten!

'Oh dear,' sighed Tortoise, puffing and panting and gasping for breath. 'If I have a little rest, perhaps I'll speed up a bit later.'

Then he tried jumping.

Tortoise carefully balanced a twig between two of the smallest toadstools he could find.

He stood back.

He lumbered forward.

With a terrific HEAVE he tried to jump! But his poor old legs just wouldn't leave the ground, and he knocked the twig off with his tummy.

'Oh dear,' he sighed again. 'If I have a little rest first, perhaps I'll get better later.'

Then he tried throwing a stone, but that was no good either.

'Oh dear,' he said, wiping his forehead with a towel, 'I don't seem to be as fit as I used to be. Perhaps I'll be better on the day.'

With that thought glowing in his mind, Tortoise plodded his weary path home to wish some more.

THE SKY WAS AS BLUE AS the sky had ever been, and the sun shone and warmed the crowds at the opening ceremony of Badger's Olympical Games.

Every single animal was there. Some to take part, and the rest to cheer them on.

In the centre of the arena, six mice—dressed in bright scarlet uniforms—raised golden trumpets to their lips and blew out a terrific fanfare that rattled and rang throughout the stadium.

TAR-AN-TAR-AN-TAR-AAAN!!!

Badger stood up on a small stage.

'Ladies and Gentleman!' he announced, when the clapping had died down. 'I bid you welcome to Badger's Olympical Games!'

There was more thunderous cheering, and Badger stood right in the middle of it all, loving every moment.

'Now is not the time,' he went on at length, 'for me to indulge in long speeches and greetifications, so I'll be brief—'

'Well said, that man!' cried Hedgehog, rather

cheekily. Badger looked at him over the top of his spectacles and sniffed.

'Let the Games . . . BEGIN!'

There was another fanfare from the mice, and clouds of butterflies were released from baskets to flutter and flit their way up into the blue.

It was a beautiful sight, and one that every animal would remember through all the days that lay ahead.

THE FIRST EVENT WAS Running. There were five animals taking part: Hare, Squirrel, Rabbit, Rat—and, of course, Tortoise.

Hare, who was the favourite, had his ears tied down with a headband.

'Lessens the wind resistance, chaps,' he announced on the starting line. 'Lets me run all the faster.'

Tortoise wasn't put off by this in the slightest. For he had something special, too. On his vest, he had stitched in big, bold letters—SUPERFAST! Just to give himself confidence. He puffed himself up a little, and felt very good indeed!

Badger—not surprisingly—was the official starter. The stadium fell silent as he raised a white flag.

'Three times round the running track,' he declared. 'On your marks . . . get set . . .'

Down came the flag.

Tortoise began to move and, to his surprise, he found his legs were going rather well.

'Must have been all that training,' he thought to himself. 'I knew I'd be better on the day.'

He looked up. There was no sign of the others.

'I—I'm even in the lead!' The thought made him smile a little smile.

Poor old Tortoise! He didn't realize that the others were already round the first bend and out of sight.

The crowd cheered and cheered and cheered and Tortoise thought it was all for him.

'If I can just keep going,' he panted, 'I'll win a medal!'

And with that, he put his head down and concentrated on plodding on as fast as he could plod.

From that moment, Tortoise looked at nothing but his feet. He didn't see the others as they sped by him once . . . and then again.

The stadium was going wild. Every single animal was on its feet, yelling and waving and clapping.

Tortoise allowed himself a quick glance up. His heart almost burst with joy as he saw, stretched across the track before him the winning tape!

With every last ounce of energy, he forced his poor old legs to move faster. The tape got nearer and nearer, and Tortoise got more and more excited!

Then suddenly, his vest—with SUPERFAST! written proudly on it—touched the white tape and broke it!

Tortoise raised his arms into the air. Hare crossed the line just behind him, followed closely by the others.

'Jolly bad luck, Hare,' gasped Tortoise, whose face had a purple tinge to it. 'I was just that bit too fast for you, eh?'

'What do you mean, old chap?' smiled Hare, who was scarcely out of puff. 'I won. We've all been round three times already—you've only gone round once!'

Tortoise swallowed hard, and his heart lurched inside him.

So he hadn't won a medal after all.

'Still, not to worry, old chap,' grinned Hare, who was really very sporting. 'You might do better in the Jumping—it's on next.'

Tortoise forced a smile to his lips and plodded

over to the jumping pit.

He had a plan. The way Tortoise saw it, he had only one chance of winning the High Jump event —and that was to wait until near the end of the competition when the bar was at its highest. He knew he hadn't the energy to do lots and lots of jumps like the others. Tortoise felt he had only one good jump in him, and if he kept it till the very end then perhaps he could surprise them all!

With a warm feeling of excitement inside him Tortoise sat down at the side of the high jump pit—waiting his moment.

It was obvious from the very start who the favourite was.

Frog!

With remarkable ease and agility, he sprang over the bar, quickly eliminating Mouse, Squirrel and Rabbit—who, although they tried very hard, were not nearly good enough.

'Higher! Higher!' cried the crowd, all of whom wanted to see just how high Frog could jump.

Badger, who was the official judge of the event, raised the bar one notch higher.

Frog yawned a little yawn, and hopped cleanly over the bar. It was just too easy for him!

'Higher! Higher!' chanted the crowd, and Badger moved the bar up again.

Once more Frog sprang forward.

Up and over he went!

Again the crowd cheered, and again the bar was put up.

And again. And again. And again.

And all the while, Tortoise watched.

And so it went on, until the bar was too high even for Frog.

This was the moment Tortoise had been waiting for.

The crowd was applauding Frog for all his efforts, and Badger was about to declare him the winner, when Tortoise stepped forward.

'Em . . . put the bar up again, please,' he said rather casually to Badger. 'I . . . I think I'd like a go.'

There was silence.

The whole stadium was astonished. They had all forgotten about Tortoise. Surely he couldn't jump higher than Frog?

There was something rather splendid in the confident way he stood there, arms folded, waiting for Badger to place the bar in position.

It was at precisely this moment that Tortoise realized just how high the bar was.

He walked forward and looked up.

And up. . . And up. . . And up.

It was way above his head! This was going to be his greatest triumph. If he could clear the bar, he'd win a medal and be the hero of Badger's Olympical Games!

Tortoise walked back twelve paces, then stood there, concentrating.

'Oh no, he's gone to sleep!' giggled Hedgehog.

'Quiet, there!' scolded Badger.

Tortoise began to rock to and fro on his feet for a few seconds, then launched himself forward.

The only sound that could be heard in the stadium was the plod, plod, plod noise of his feet as he went faster and faster, until he was going as fast as he could go!

When he was right in front of the bar, Tortoise closed his eyes and jumped with all his might!

He sailed through the air, and flopped down into the warm, soft sand of the jumping pit!

He looked up. The bar was still there! He'd cleared it! He'd soared right over it!

Tortoise stood up and raised his arms aloft to the cheering crowds!

It was only after a couple of minutes that he realized something terrible. They weren't cheering. They were laughing! The entire stadium was in fits of laughter!

Badger came over.

'Bad luck, Tortoise,' he said, trying hard not to laugh himself. 'I'm afraid you didn't quite clear the bar—you shot right underneath the thing!'

And with that, Badger clutched his sides, threw his head back, and simply roared with laughter!

It was rather rude of them all to make fun of poor old Tortoise like that, but it had been a very funny sight!

It was no joke for Tortoise. For the second time that day, he felt a sense of failure seep through him. He sank down into the sand and sat there for a long, long time.

TORTOISE WOULD HAVE sat in the jumping pit for ever if it hadn't been for Badger announcing that the next event was Throwing the Stone, and would all those who had entered this competition make their way to the specially fenced-off area 'without further pausifications'.

Tortoise stood up and brushed the sand from the seat of his shorts.

Although he was very down-hearted when he set off, by the time he arrived he had cheered up quite a bit.

After all, he had as good a chance as anybody else!

It seemed easy enough. All the competitors had to do was to pick up a stone, stand at the line, and throw it. Whoever threw it the farthest won the medal.

Squirrel looked easily the best. It wasn't really surprising; every autumn he spent hours on end throwing big bags of nuts up into a hole in his tree to keep him in food for the winter.

He picked up the stone, tucked it under his chin, spun round once and launched it into the air with a magnificent push.

It was as if the stone had wings. It flew through the air and landed well beyond the little flags which showed how far the others had thrown.

There was only one competitor to go after Squirrel.

And that was Tortoise.

This, he decided, was his chance. He'd show them all. He'd give them something to cheer this time.

The stadium was quiet. Every eye was on Tortoise as he walked slowly over to the line.

He bent down to pick up the stone. It was heavier than he thought, but this made him all the more determined to win.

Tortoise tucked the stone under his chin, the way he'd seen Squirrel do it.

Then he spun round once.

Then twice.

Then three times . . . then four times . . .

By the time he'd spun round eleven times, Tortoise realized to his horror that he couldn't stop! And at exactly the same moment it dawned on the crowd that something peculiar was happening.

One by one, they began to smile . . . then giggle . . . then chortle . . . then chuckle . . . and then howl with laughter at the sight of Tortoise spinning round and round in the centre of the stadium.

Round and round he went, and louder and louder grew the laughter.

Then, suddenly, the stone shot from his hand, flew straight up in the air, and landed with a terrible thud—right on his toes!

Tortoise stopped spinning immediately, and fell in a heap on the ground.

All the animals in the stadium were crying with laughter. All the animals but poor old Tortoise!

He had tears in his eyes all right. But they weren't tears of laughter.

With his foot throbbing, and his head spinning, Tortoise limped and staggered his way out of the stadium.

When he was quite sure that he was alone and that no one could see him, he crawled into some long grass and cried.

A THOUSAND TEARDROPS LATER, Tortoise stopped sobbing. He heard voices. It was Badger, and lots of other animals. Tortoise poked his head through a clump of ferns. Lined up in a long row in front of his very eyes were mice, and rabbits, and rats, and moles, and squirrels, and hares. There must have been a score or more. They were all wearing skis.

It took Tortoise a minute or so to realize that he'd hobbled right up the slope to the starting point of the Ski-ing Down the Muddy Hill event.

Again Badger was the Official Starter.

'Remember,' he shouted through a megaphone, 'you go right down the slope, keeping between the flags as you descendify. First across the line in the centre of the stadium is the winner.'

He raised the starting pistol.

'On your marks . . .'

Tortoise leaned forward a little to watch.

'Get set . . .'

Tortoise leaned forward a little more.

BANG ! ! ! went Badger's starting gun.

Tortoise almost jumped right out of his shell! He felt his feet slither and slip on the damp grass, and before he knew what was happening, he tumbled out of his hidey-hole and landed upside-down on the starting line!

In an instant, he began to slide down the hill after the skiers!

You should have seen him, waving his arms and his legs in the air as he gathered speed.

Bumpity-bump! Thumpity-thump! Clumpity-clump! Down he went, bouncing and bobbing, sliding and slithering—completely out of control!

And you should have seen the looks on the faces of the other animals as Tortoise zoomed through them, mud spraying up behind as he shot away!

And you should have seen him as he came hurtling down between the flags at breakneck speed until he swooshed across the winning line and came to a halt right in the centre of the stadium!

The crowd went mad!

They cheered and roared and yelled and screamed and chanted Tortoise's name.

'We love you, Tortoise! We love you, Tortoise!'

He stood up in the centre of the arena and thought his heart was going to burst with joy!

Tortoise could hardly believe it was happening to him.

He was still in a daze at the closing ceremony that night when, beneath a beautiful golden moon, Badger presented the medals.

To Hare for the Running.

To Frog for the Jumping.

To Squirrel for Throwing the Stone.

And to Tortoise for Ski-ing Down the Muddy Slope.

And as each winner leaned forward to have the medal hung round his neck, the six mice—dressed in bright scarlet uniforms—trumpeted out their praise.

As the last notes from the final fanfare bounced away into the forest, Tortoise looked up at the sky, and sighed with pure happiness.

Hedgehog's Magic
Wishing Ring

THE FOREST WAS QUIET AGAIN. For four whole days, the north wind had been trapped in the clearing and, like a wild horse, had tossed and charged and stamped and reared, looking for an escape.

But try as it could, there was no way out.

Just when it seemed as if it was to be harnessed for ever, it found a weakness in an old, diseased elm tree and had thrashed it to the ground without mercy.

In a single leap, the wild wind cleared the dead, grey branches and was gone.

The forest was quiet again.

Then, from below the fallen elm tree, from a little bed of rolled-up moss and leaves, there came a strange, tuneless humming noise.

'Tum-te-tum-te-tiddley-toe
I thought that wind would never go!'

It was Hedgehog, who for reasons best known to himself, had taken to speaking in rhyme—

all of the time—

in manner sublime . . .

come rain or come shine . . .

if you see what I mean.

He stretched himself and looked about him with his blackberry eyes and sniffed.

All around were new smells. Fresh smells. Lovely rich smells of acorns and beech nuts and beautiful berries.

'Tum-te-tum-te-tiddley-tee

Lots of lovely food for me!'

Hedgehog pulled on his wellies, wound a scarf around his neck and off he went, tunelessly humming his way through the wind-trampled undergrowth.

All morning he snuffled and sniffled about, investigating this, rummaging through that, all the while, making up silly little songs to sing.

'Tum-te-tum-te-tiddley-ty

Oh, how I love an apple pie!

Tum-te-tum-te-tiddley-too

Oh, how I love a bramble stew!'

Then, suddenly, in a quiet little corner of the forest, sheltered by a frail screen of ferns, on a deep-piled carpet of moss, was something that put all thoughts of singing clean out of his head. Something that made his heart bump and thump inside him, like rabbits rushing down a burrow!

There before him was a tiny circle of mushrooms—a fairy circle, a magic ring!

Hedgehog could hardly believe it. He'd often heard tales of magic rings, and how if you stood in the middle of one, and wished a wish, it would come true.

He'd often heard the tales, but he never thought that it would happen to him!

But it had—it really had!

He dipped the toe of his right welly into the circle, then he put his whole boot in, then he pulled the other foot in after him and there he was standing slap-bang in the middle of a magic wishing ring!

There was a flash, a pop, and there before him, dripping stars, was the Fairy Hedgehog herself!

Hedgehog gaped.

She was beautiful! Well, maybe not quite beautiful, for her crown was ever so slightly bashed and her magic wand had been snapped at one time and was bound together with string.

But she was really there, and that was all that mattered to Hedgehog.

He just gaped and gaped and gaped.

'Well then, dearie,' said the Fairy Hedgehog, 'and what's it to be then?'

Hedgehog opened his mouth, but the words seemed stuck to his tongue.

'C'mon, c'mon now, dearie—I haven't got all day, you know. Honestly, the amount of work I've got just now, you'd hardly believe it!'

Hedgehog tried to speak again, but although his lips moved, the words wouldn't come out!

The Fairy Hedgehog sighed, looked skywards, then began to inspect her fingernails.

'Right,' she said, 'I'll count up to three. If you haven't decided what you want by the time I count to three, you've had it! I'm not standing about here all day waiting for you to speak. One—two—'

Just as she was on the point of saying three, the words came pouring out!

'Could . . . could it be for two?' he blurted out. 'You see, I've got a friend, Tortoise, and I'd like my wish to be for him too. Could it? Could it? Oh, please . . .'

The Fairy Hedgehog—who wasn't as patient as Hedgehog thought she should have been—threw her hands up in the air.

'Dear, oh, dear!' she exclaimed. 'First he keeps me waiting, then he asks for a double helping!'

She shook her head and tutted. 'Oh, well, I suppose. Close your eyes and wish and I'll see what I can do. Anything for a quiet life!'

Hedgehog closed his eyes as tight as he could and wished. The Fairy Hedgehog boinked him with her wand and a huge cluster of stars burst all around them.

'Right, that's your lot—I'm off to get my feet up!' she said. And she disappeared in a puff of blue smoke!

Hedgehog stood in the centre of the ring, and for a couple of minutes did nothing. Then he looked about him and frowned, and blinked, and scratched his head, and wondered if it had really happened.

Had his wish come true? Should he try and see if it had?

No. Maybe he'd better wait until he told Tortoise. After all, it was for them both.

Tortoise was busy clearing some leaves and twigs from his doorstep when Hedgehog came rushing up.

'I've seen her!' he yelled from the foot of the path. 'Tortoise! I've seen her, and she touched me with her wand, and it's for us both!'

Tortoise smiled and shook his head.

'I—I'm not quite with you, Hedgehog,' he said.

'Seen who? What's for us both?'

'The Fairy Hedgehog! She granted me a wish, and it's for both of us!'

Tortoise was still baffled. Was this another of Hedgehog's crazy jokes, the sort he was always making? And yet, it didn't seem like a joke. Hedgehog sounded most sincere.

'Come on!' he cried, pulling at Tortoise's sleeve. 'We must go to the clearing and show Badger and the others! It's amazing—what a wish! And it's for us both!'

'But—but what on earth did you wish for?' asked Tortoise.

Hedgehog's face almost split in two with the biggest grin he'd ever grinned.

'I'll whisper!' he said, his eyes twinkling. He looked over his shoulder to make sure that no one else was about, then he spoke in low and secret tones.

Tortoise almost fell over!

'You did what?' he gasped. 'You can what? We can what?' His voice got higher and higher.

'Yes, it's true!' said Hedgehog. 'Isn't it fun! Come on, let's go to the clearing and show them all!'

In the middle of the clearing, there was a clump of foxgloves, and near them was a tree trunk.

Hedgehog climbed up on top of it, then gave Tortoise a helping heave up beside him.

Then they both took a deep breath and yelled out loud.

'Badger! Oh, Badger! Come and see us! Come and see what we can do!'

For a long time, nothing happened, but then a snout appeared from Badger's doorway. It was followed by a head, and then a body, and finally a whole Badger emerged.

He pushed his spectacles up his snout and peered through them.

'What's all this then?' he asked. 'What's all the noisification?'

Hedgehog and Tortoise were almost bursting at the seams with excitement.

'Oh, Badger?' cried Hedgehog. 'I stood in the mushrooms and she touched me with her wand, and—and—'

By this time, a whole crowd of creatures had gathered to see what the fuss was about.

Moles and rabbits and squirrels and mice and all sorts milled around.

Badger turned to Squirrel, tapping the side of his head with his forefinger.

'He's quite mad! Always thought it, mind you. His eyes have that sort of stupidating look about them!'

Squirrel nodded, but Hedgehog wasn't finished.

'No!' he yelled. 'It's true. Do you know what we can do?'

Badger felt a laugh tugging at the corners of his mouth, but he tried hard and kept it in. He shook his head.

'We,' cried Hedgehog, 'we can FLY!'

That was it! The laugh tugged hard and burst forth from Badger. And at the same time the rest of the creatures threw their heads back too and howled and howled.

Hedgehog ignored them all. Without a word, he held out his arms, leaned forward and dived off the tree stump.

For a split second, it seemed as if he was going to fall flat on his face, but amazingly he levelled off and soared up into the sky!

The laughter stopped immediately. There was a gasp from the assembled animals. Open mouthed they stared upwards.

Above them, Hedgehog giggled for all he was worth.

'Your turn, Tortoise!' he called down to the tiny figure below him.

All eyes turned to Tortoise as he too held out his arms. He gave a little jump. There was another gasp as he floated up into the air!

Up and up and up and up!

Every single animal of the forest and the woodlands stood pop-eyed in the clearing.

They pinched themselves. They blinked. They rubbed their eyes, and looked away, and then looked back. But no matter what they did—nothing changed. Hedgehog and Tortoise were flying!

The pair of them climbed high on the breezes, so high that they could almost tickle the tummies

of the big fleecy clouds.

Then they swooped down in a steep glide.

Down and down and down they dived, with the wind rushing and tugging at them as they zoomed earthwards.

Nearer and nearer and nearer they got to the crowd of creatures in the clearing.

Mice and rabbits and squirrels, and even Badger himself, hurled themselves to the ground.

At the very last moment, the pair straightened out, skimming over the grass, laughing and shrieking as they went.

'Told you!' yelled Hedgehog as they shot past. 'I told you we could fly!'

And fly they did—loops and turns and spirals and glides and dives and somersaults in the air. And on the ground below the assembled animals were amazed at it all. Time and time again they clapped and cheered each daring manoeuvre.

'Splendestible brain, that Hedgehog has,' said Badger. 'I've always thought that. And Tortoise— he's a genius.'

The words were scarcely out of Badger's mouth when disaster struck!

In the middle of a high-speed streak across the tree-tops, Hedgehog and Tortoise collided in mid-air.

With a tremendous clatter, they walloped full into each other and tumbled down, bouncing and battering off branches before thumping hard upon the ground.

Some of the creatures screamed, some covered their eyes, then they all rushed forward.

When Hedgehog came to, the first thing he heard was Badger.

'Give him air! Give him air!' he was saying as he ushered the assembled animals back a bit.

Hedgehog felt something cold on his brow, and he opened his eyes.

Tortoise was bending over him, dabbing his forehead with a moist handkerchief.

'Tortoise!' gasped Hedgehog. 'Are you all right?'

Tortoise frowned.

'What do you mean, am I all right? *You're* the one who was knocked out!'

Hedgehog sat up.

'But—' he began.

'Take it easy, old friend,' went on Tortoise. 'A bump on the head can be a nasty thing, you know. The wind blew down your elm tree this morning and a branch struck you on the head!'

Hedgehog rubbed the bump, and Tortoise continued.

'You've been out cold most of the day!'

'Yes,' chuckled Badger. 'And dreaming by the sound of it, too. Some nonsensicals about flying!'

Hedgehog struggled to his feet.

'But I can fly!' he insisted. 'The Fairy Hedgehog . . .'

Before anyone could stop him, he held out his arms and dived forwards.

Poor old Hedgehog—with a terrible thud, he fell flat on his face!

So he couldn't fly. It had all been a dream.

With a heavy heart, he walked slowly away from the clearing, to be alone for a while. To turn things over. To think things out.

And after he had walked and thought and walked and thought and walked a little more, he stopped.

Suddenly.

For there, in a quiet little corner of the forest, sheltered by a frail screen of ferns, was a tiny circle of mushrooms!

Hedgehog's heart began to thump and bump inside him.

Fire, Fire!

IT WAS A DAY FOR doing very little.

'Or even less,' thought Tortoise to himself as he snuggled in the warmth of the mossy bank at the edge of the clearing deep in the forest in the middle of a sunny day.

Above him, a clump of foxgloves nodded their pretty purple heads in the soft summer breeze, and two butterflies dipped and danced for a moment between them.

Beside him, basking in the sunshine in a pair of flowery shorts that were three sizes too big, was Hedgehog. He'd covered his snout with a red polka-dot handkerchief to give himself some shade and it billowed and flopped . . . billowed and flopped . . . billowed and flopped in time to the snores that came from him.

'Eeeh, it's all right for some!' said a voice from behind the foxgloves.

Tortoise thought hard, but he couldn't quite guess who it was.

He opened one eye, but he couldn't quite see who it was.

So he opened both eyes and blinked.

It was Squirrel.

'I said it's all right for some,' he repeated. 'You pair, you've done nowt but sunbathe for a whole fortnight. Eeeh, just look at the state of you, lad!'

He tapped Hedgehog with his foot.

'Wakey-wakey, Sleepyhead!'

The red polka-dot handkerchief continued to billow and flop . . . billow and flop . . .

Squirrel shook his head. Then a gleam like the first star of a winter's night came into his eye.

'Hey up, Hedgehog!' he cried suddenly. 'Your shorts are on fire!'

There was a loud grunt and a yell, and the red polka-dot handkerchief sailed high into the air as Hedgehog beat his hands up and down.

'Eeeh, fooled you there, lad!' laughed Squirrel, slinging a sack over his shoulder and skipping away.

Hedgehog drummed his fingers on a stone and waited till Squirrel was almost out of sight.

'Hey, Squirrel!' he called. 'Come here a minute! It's important! Honest!'

Back skipped Squirrel, still chuckling at his joke.

Hedgehog let him come all the way over to the mossy bank.

All the way over.

Then he giggled.

'Nuts to you!' he declared simply, placing the red polka-dot handkerchief back over his snout as he lay down.

Squirrel, who was a good-natured creature, laughed again and was gone.

Tortoise said nothing.

How could he?

He was asleep.

SQUIRREL WAS A WORKER, there was no denying it.

He spent nearly all summer and autumn collecting sackloads of food to keep him going through the long winter days. During the recent hot spell, he'd discovered the perfect way to get his bag filled.

Each day, he made his way to the part of the forest that was a picnic area for people. All he had to do was to scamper up and down a couple of trees and do a few skips about on the grass, and pretty soon every little boy and girl in the picnic area would bring him titbits of food.

Apple-cores, peanuts, crisps and crusts, acorns, beechnuts, anything and everything. There wasn't a soul who could resist the friendly little Squirrel, and it took hardly any time at all to fill up his sack.

But this particular summer's day, when the forest was full with a million humming insects and a thousand singing birds, the bag was to remain empty.

Something happened.

Something terrible happened.

TORTOISE AND HEDGEHOG WERE still sound asleep when Squirrel came rushing back.

'Fire! Fire!' he squealed.

Tortoise and Hedgehog groaned.

'Come off it, Squirrel—once a day's enough for all that sort of rubbish!'

'No! No!' cried Squirrel. 'One of the people threw away a little firestick. It landed on some dry grass. It's spreading and it's coming this way! Eeeh, look!'

Tortoise and Hedgehog looked.

Above the trees at the far side of the clearing, there was a long plume of smoke. It was like the big, bushy tail of some evil creature as it swished angrily back and forth in the sky, spanning the whole width of the forest.

And to make matters worse, the freshening breeze was bringing it closer to them!

For a moment, the three animals said nothing.

'Come on!' they all yelled at once. 'We must warn Badger and the others!'

'I'm coming! I'm coming!' Badger muttered. 'No need for all this noisification! Can't a person get any sleep around here?'

Squirrel and Hedgehog and Tortoise kept on knocking and hammering and pounding till Badger appeared.

'The forest's on fire! The forest's on fire!'

Badger looked at the three frantic creatures on his doorstep, then followed their jabbing fingers to

53

the swelling smoke above the trees.

His eyes opened wide with horror.

Badger, who was a brilliant organizer, summed up the situation immediately.

'We must all get out of the forest,' he said without fuss. Then he turned and ran in his lumbering, stiff-legged manner into his house. There was a clattering and a banging and a crashing noise as he rummaged around in one of his cupboards.

In a moment, he returned with a megaphone in one hand and a bright yellow helmet in the other.

He plonked the helmet on his head, tapped it down and climbed up onto a tree stump in the middle of the clearing.

'Attention, all animals of the forest!' he shouted through the megaphone, his voice booming and echoing. 'Attention, please!'

Moles, rabbits, hares, rats, frogs, and mice and all sorts popped their noses and snouts and whiskers out of their homes in burrows and scrapes and holes and hollows.

'The forest's on fire!' declared Badger. 'We'll have to make escapations without pausification!'

One of the animals, I think it was Mrs. Dormouse, gave a little squeak, and several others began to murmur in frightened whimpers.

Badger held his hand on high.

'Now I want everyone to keep his—or her, whichever is appropriable—I want everyone to keep his or her head. There's no need for panication. It might be just a little fire, and the people might well be able to deal with it. But to be on the

55

safe side, I think it would be wise if we were to—er—um—'

Badger stroked his chin as he thought of one of his special words.

'Scarper!' yelled Hedgehog.

And they all agreed.

WITHIN MOMENTS THE animals had begun to evacuate their homes.

Cases, and crates, and boxes, and bags were quickly crammed with prize possessions. Wheelbarrows were laden high with tottering towers of worldly goods.

Hedgehog, who didn't have too many worldly goods, tied a few odds and ends and an apple in his red polka-dot handkerchief and joined Tortoise, who took only the gold medal which he'd once won in the Games, and which was very dear to him.

Badger took nothing at all—except for his megaphone and his bright yellow helmet—having decided that he'd have his hands full enough keeping everyone under control.

He strode to the head of the column of creatures.

'Is everyone readified?'

There was a cry of anguish from Mrs. Rabbit.

She and her husband had lined up their entire family in a long row outside their burrow.

'We're still counting!' she wailed. 'Fourteen . . . fifteen . . . sixteen . . . seventeen . . . and Daddy makes eighteen . . . yes! Yes! All present and correct! Ready now!'

Badger waved his arm in a circle through the air and pointed dramatically ahead.

'Operation Escapation!' he declared grandly.

The long column of creatures began to move forward.

Behind them, feeding greedily on the dry grass and leaves, and ferns, and bushes, and branches, and trees, the hungry forest fire crept nearer.

THE GOING WAS ROUGH and heavy and slow.

Badger did his best to keep everyone moving, but it was a difficult task. Wheels came off wheelbarrows, bags burst open and boxes spilled over, scattering their contents among the undergrowth.

When this happened, everything would grind to a halt as everybody flocked round to pick up as much as they could. But the roar of the fire was getting louder and louder, and the long, grey fingers of smoke were already reaching through the trees towards them!

'We must keep going!' boomed Badger through the megaphone. 'If we stop now the fire will get us and we'll all be scorchified!'

Again the column would creep forward.

But then they'd find a stream to cross, or an old fallen tree would block their path and they'd have to scramble the long way round.

And all the while, the forest fire crackled nearer. It had already blazed across their clearing and had taken away all trace of the mossy bank where Tortoise and Hedgehog had been sunning themselves not so long ago. The beautiful purple foxgloves had curtsied silently into the flames and were gone.

And there was no sign at all of the dancing butterflies.

The animals stumbled on.

Then, after a score or more times of stopping and picking things up, and sharing loads, and checking to make sure everyone was there, Squirrel gave a sudden cry.

'Eeeh! Look! Up ahead! There's daylight—we've reached the edge of the forest!'

A triumphant cheer echoed all around.

'Hurrah! Hurrah! Well done, Badger! You've saved us all!'

And each and every one of them found fresh strength and energy to surge forward, clear of the burning woods.

Where the trees stopped, the ground fell away in a long, gentle slope.

Before them rolled a sea of dry grass, which rustled and whispered like waves, and every now and then revealed flashes of poppies and ox-eye daisies and yellow ragwort.

Beyond the grass rose rushes and taller reeds, and beyond the taller reeds, glinting like an evil eye, was a fat, grey river.

It curled in a huge, horseshoe loop in front of them. It was big and wide and deep, and moved without sound, like a bad dream.

The animals stopped their cheering and looked at each other.

Although no words were spoken, each and every one of them knew what the others were thinking.

They weren't safe at all.

They were trapped.

There was no way of getting across the river, and there was no way back, for the fire had already cut off their retreat as it came roaring and crunching onwards, spitting great showers of sparks high into the blackened sky.

And the wind was still freshening.

Already the animals could smell the smoke, and hear the crackle, and feel the heat, and taste the ashes.

Some began to cry and look wildly about them. There was no escape.

Badger held his hand high to keep things calm, but even he could find no words of comfort, no reassurance.

They were all trapped.

There was nothing they could do but wait.

THE IDEA CAME TO Tortoise like a shaft of golden sunlight burning through a misty autumn morning.

'There is a way,' he told Badger. 'But we must be quick.'

He drew a sketch on the ground with a pointed twig.

'That's the river, and there's the line of the fire, and that's us stuck in the middle.'

Badger frowned, he knew all this, but Tortoise had a strange, inspired look about him, so he let him go on.

'The wind's getting stronger by the minute, so if we were to set fire to the grass between us and the river, it would burn away from us before the big fire gets here!'

Badger nodded, and Tortoise continued.

'Then, once the dry grass and reeds have burned away, we dig a huge underground hole in the middle and wait till the big fire burns itself out. It shouldn't come near us, because it can't burn what's already burnt!'

Badger was silent for a moment as he thought over the plan. Then he drew in a deep breath and gave out a terrific roar that made every single animal jump—especially Tortoise, who was nearest and who nearly popped right out of his shell!

'Brilliant, Tortoise! Splendestible stuff! And after the fire's gone, we dig ourselves out then go off to find a new forest somewhere else! You marvellistic little fellow!'

There was hope, and Badger was in control again. He organized the excited animals as if the idea had been all his own.

'What we need is someone speedy to volunteerify himself—Hare, you'll do!'

Hare stepped forward.

'And you, Squirrel,' went on Badger, 'go and fetch a bundle of dry grass to use as a torch.'

Squirrel did so, and in a moment Hare was off on his mission.

He sped back to the advancing flames to light the torch.

Three times he tried, and three times the fierce heat drove him back.

The others watched, gasping at his heroic efforts. Then, just when it seemed as if Hare would have to give up, he tried once more and this time —the torch was lit!

Hare turned and streaked towards the dry

grass. He raced along the edge, setting fire to the grass every few metres.

In an instant, the reeds and rushes and tinder-dry grasses were ablaze!

Hare shot back to a hero's welcome.

As Tortoise had predicted, the wind drove the fire swiftly through the dry grass—away from the animals, towards the river.

Within seconds, the whole lot was reduced to ashes, and the greedy flames spluttered and sizzled out at the water's edge.

Badger and the others looked back over their shoulders. The snarling forest fire was much closer now, and the smoke streaming through the

wood towards them!

Every few seconds, above the roar, they could hear crashing noises, like giant's footsteps, and a million sparks would spray up into the black, belching smoke as yet another tree toppled down into the flames.

'Quickly!' yelled Badger through the megaphone. 'It's time for the moles to do their bit. By the left . . . quick march!'

A squad of a dozen moles, with picks and shovels over their shoulders, marched into the middle of the newly burnt-out patch.

The scorched earth was still hot from the fire, but the moles felt nothing through the thick, hobnailed soles of their working boots. In no time at all, they began to dig.

Beads of sweat bounced off their brows and the muscles of their thick arms strained and rippled away as great clods of earth flew into the air.

The soil near the river was soft and easy to dig and it wasn't long before the moles disappeared below the ground.

Badger and the rest waited anxiously at the edge of the forest. The flames were very close now. Huge lumps of burning branches were falling around them.

The animals coughed and spluttered as the cruel smoke got into their nostrils and made their eyes nip and run with tears.

One of Mrs. Rabbit's youngsters strayed from the group and was only just plucked to safety by Badger as a flaming chestnut tree roared down in a cascade of sparks.

Then, suddenly, one of the moles appeared at the mouth of the hole. He waved his shovel triumphantly in the air.

The signal!

Grabbing what they could of their possessions, the animals poured out of the burning woods and down into the tunnel.

The moles had done a brilliant job! The en-

trance was long and narrow, like the neck of a
bottle. Then it opened out to form a huge underground cavern, providing enough room for all the
animals.

As the last creature scrambled in, the tunnel
mouth was sealed off, and the long wait began.

INSIDE THE CHAMBER, the animals huddled
together round the flickering light of a single
lantern.

Above the ground, they could hear the rumble
and the roar of the forest fire, and the crunch and
thump of falling trees and branches.

Suddenly, Badger had an idea.

'A song!' he cried. 'What we need is a song!
Mrs. Mouse—you can start us off!'

Mrs. Mouse jumped up nervously, her fingers
fidgeting away as if she was knitting with neither
needles nor wool.

'Me? Sing? I can't sing—me? Oh dear, what
shall I sing anyway? Oh dear!'

'What about "Nuts and Berries and Acorns"?'
suggested Badger. 'You commencify, and we'll all
join in the chorusy bits!'

'Nuts and Berries and Acorns' is a favourite
song among the animals. The words are simple,

67

and they make up the tune as they go along. Someone sings the first line, then all join in to sing 'Nuts
and berries and acorns'—nothing to it at all.

Mrs. Mouse smiled a bashful little smile, looked
quickly about her, then began to sing in her high,
soprano voice.

> *This is the tale of a little mouse*
> *Nuts and berries and acorns!*
> *She ran away from her little house*
> *Nuts and berries and acorns!*
> *She ran away but at half-past three*
> *A very, very hungry little mouse was she*
> *She was home in time for tea*
> *Nuts and berries and acorns!*

Then one of the moles stood up and sang in a
rich, mellow bass voice that echoed all around the
cavern.

> *This is the tale of a little mole*
> *Nuts and berries and acorns!*
> *He ran away from his little hole*
> *Nuts and berries and acorns!*
> *He ran away but at half-past three*
> *A very, very hungry little mole was he*
> *He was home in time for tea*
> *Nuts and berries and acorns!*

Then it was the turn of Squirrel, a fine tenor.

> *This is the tale of a squirrel grey*
> *Nuts and berries and acorns!*
> *He ran away from his home one day*
> *Nuts and berries and acorns!*
> *He ran away but at half-past three*
> *A very, very hungry little squirrel was he*
> *He was home in time for tea*
> *Nuts and berries and acorns!*

And finally, Badger rose and sang his verse with great gusto—but little regard for music, tone or rhythm.

> *This is the tale of a badger gay*
> *Nuts and berries and acorns!*
> *He ran away from his home one day*
> *Nuts and berries and acorns!*
> *He ran away but at half-past three*
> *A very, very hungry little badger was he*
> *He was home in time for tea*
> *Nuts and berries and acorns!*

The song finished with a tremendous cheer, and Badger holding grimly on to the last note. Then he dived into a superb bow and surfaced a full minute later, beaming.

'Splendestible!' he sighed. 'Now, would anyone else care to make a contribulation?'

Hedgehog was on his feet in a flash.

'I've got a terrific joke to tell you,' he chuckled.

There was a loud groan from everyone. Hedgehog's jokes were well known for being particularly strange. He enjoyed them, but hardly anyone else understood what he found so funny. But that didn't trouble Hedgehog, and there was no stopping him.

'Well,' he said, already giggling. 'There was this little mouse, see? And she met two snakes—adders, they were. Well—' he broke off to wipe a tear of laughter from his eye—'Well, one of the snakes never ate her—but the adder adder adder!'

Hedgehog clutched at his sides and fell into a helpless heap of giggles.

'Adder adder adder?' queried Badger. 'Thought you said there were two snakes—adder adder adder makes three!'

'No—no!' howled Hedgehog. 'The adder adder adder—the other adder had her—adder adder adder—get it? Eh?'

And again he fell down and rolled about laughing.

Badger frowned and muttered something.

'And *I* don't think that's very funny!' protested Mrs. Mouse.

'Oh, never mind then,' groaned Hedgehog, mopping his brow with his red polka-dot handkerchief. 'I've got an even better one for you. What happened when the frog broke down? Eh? Tell me that then? What happened when the Frog broke down? He had to get Toad home! Get it? Toad—towed—he had to get Toad home!'

And yet again, Hedgehog wriggled about on the floor, laughing his head off at his own joke.

He was greeted with a chorus of boos and hisses and a few shouts of 'Gerroff!'

A hazelnut whistled past his nose, so he curled up into a ball and remained like that for quite some time.

Badger stood up, shook his head and sighed.

'Well, let's have no more of such nonsensicals. What about a story—and what better tale is there than the one about how Tortoise won that gold medal of his!'

'Rubbish!' muttered Hedgehog from inside his ball, but he was drowned by a burst of applause and cheering from everyone else.

'Come on, then, Tortoise, wherever you are,' said Badger, peering into the gloom. 'Let's hear it from you!'

But there was no reply from Tortoise.

A chill of dreadful horror shivered through the chamber as the animals, snuggling safe below the forest fire, realized that Tortoise wasn't with them.

And if he wasn't with them—that could mean only one thing. That he was above the ground!

And if he was above the ground—that, too, could mean only one thing . . .

The animals sat in silence as they listened to the crackling of the flames above them.

A LONG AND LONELY TIME LATER, when Badger had decided that it was safe to go above the ground, the moles unsealed the entrance.

The fire had burnt itself out, just as Tortoise had said it would.

Charred and blackened trees stood stark against a dull grey sky that still hung heavy with smoke. Cinders and ashes lay thick on the ground like banks of drifted snow.

And all around them was silence. No bees buzzed, no insects hummed, no birds sang.

Badger climbed wearily on to a stone and addressed the assembled animals. A large tear swelled in the corner of his eye and wobbled down his snout.

Hedgehog's red polka-dot handkerchief felt cold and chill against his cheek.

Badger coughed as the taste of smoke caught at the back of his throat. With a trembling hand, he removed his helmet.

'Ladies and gentlemen,' he began. 'It would appear that the plan thought up by dear old Tortoise has worked. We're all safe, as he told us we would be. All of us, that is, except one . . .'

Another tear swelled and rolled out.

'What a catastrible that the hero of the hour, the aforementionated Tortoise, should be lost to us. When we reach our new forest, as I'm sure we all will, we shall build a statue of him, as a memorification. Because if it hadn't been for dear old—'

Badger stopped speaking in mid-sentence. He wobbled and almost fell from the stone.

Then, to his utter and absolute astonishment, he wobbled again!

The stone he was standing on was moving!

Badger stepped down and the whole crowd of creatures gasped as, slowly but surely, the stone stood up!

But wait—it wasn't a stone!

It was . . . it was . . .

'Tortoise!' roared Badger in disbelief. 'We all thought you'd been—been—'

'And I thought so too!' cried Tortoise, so happy to see all his friends again. 'But just as we were all going into the tunnel, I realized my medal had dropped off. It took me ages to find it, and when I eventually did, the smoke was so thick that I couldn't see where you'd all gone! So I just crawled into the middle of the bit we'd set fire to and hid in my shell! And jolly hot it was, too, I can tell you!'

In an instant, everyone was clamouring round

him, patting him and dusting the ash from his back, and laughing and dancing and jumping just for the sheer pleasure it gave them!

Tortoise was safe—they all were!

Just then, as if by magic, a single sunbeam stole through the smoke and for a brief moment, far in the distance, they could see their new wood.

And they were all still singing when they reached there that night.

The End